If your child struggles with a word, you can encourage "sounding it out," but keep in mind that not all words can be sounded out. Your child might pick up clues about a word from the picture, other words in the sentence, or any rhyming patterns. If your child struggles with a word for more than five seconds, it is usually best to simply say the word.

Most of all, remember to praise your child's efforts and keep the reading fun. After you have finished the book, ask a few questions and discuss what you have read together. Rereading this book multiple times may also be helpful for your child.

Try to keep the tips above in mind as you read together, but don't worry about doing everything right. Simply sharing the enjoyment of reading together will increase your child's reading skills and help to start your child off on a lifetime of reading enjoyment!

The New Tribe

A We Both Read® Book

Welcome to the world, Ellington Tucker Kai Mitchell.
Wondrous things await you!
—J. C.

Text Copyright © 2005 by Jana Carson
Illustrations Copyright © 2005 by Meryl Treatner

Originally published as Stop Teasing Taylor.

We Both Read® is a trademark of Treasure Bay, Inc.

Published by Treasure Bay, Inc.
P.O. Box 119
Novato, CA 94948 USA

Printed in Singapore

Library of Congress Catalog Card Number: 2011944944

Hardcover ISBN: 978-1-60115-263-3
Paperback ISBN: 978-1-60115-264-0

We Both Read® Books
Patent No. 5,957,693

Visit us online at:
www.WeBothRead.com

PR-1-12

WE BOTH READ®

The New Tribe

By Jana Carson

Illustrated by Meryl Treatner

TREASURE BAY

It was the night before the first day of school and I was so **excited!** I laid out my new school clothes and packed all my new school supplies into my brand new backpack. I wanted everything to be perfect for tomorrow.

"Otis," my mom called, "it's time to get ready for bed!"

But I was too **excited** to go to bed. I asked
my mom if I could call my best friend. She said
it was okay.

I knew **Taylor's** phone number by heart because **Taylor** and I had been best friends since pre-school. But when I finished dialing, a woman came on the phone and told me, "This number is no longer in service."

I was confused. I asked my mom why **Taylor's** phone wasn't working right.

Mom didn't know why it wasn't working. But she did know that it was time for bed now. I would just have to talk to **Taylor** in the morning.

I went to bed and finally drifted off to sleep, thinking about the first day of school. I **wondered** if Taylor would be in my class. I really **hoped** my teacher would be nice. I was pretty sure that the first day of school was going to be great.

I waited at the bus stop with my dad. I
wondered why the bus was so late. I **hoped**
Taylor was on the bus.

When the bus finally arrived, I climbed aboard and quickly searched through all of the familiar faces until I found the one that I liked best.

"Hey, Taylor!" I shouted to my friend.

"Hey, Otis!" he shouted back with a great big smile.

Miss King was waiting for us at school. She told me that I was in her class. She told Taylor he was in her class too. It was going to be a great first day of school!

 Then I noticed that Taylor was wearing his old clothes and was carrying the same backpack he had last year.

"Where's your new stuff?" I asked.

Before Taylor could answer, two girls **pointed** at his feet and **laughed**. "Look!" they said. "Taylor has a hole in his shoe!"

More kids came to look at Taylor's shoe. They all **laughed** and **pointed.**

I wanted to help Taylor. But I didn't know what to do.

It was terrible. And just when I thought that things couldn't get any worse, they did. An older boy **shouted,** "Cry baby! Cry baby!" and Taylor started to cry.

I had to do something fast!

I **shouted** for them to stop! I shouted as loud as I could!

Miss King heard all the noise and rushed over.

"Otis and Taylor, please stay outside with me," she instructed. "The rest of you kids go into the classroom."

She asked us what happened and Taylor was so upset that he couldn't talk. So I said, "We're having a very *bad* first day of school."

I told Miss King that the kids were saying mean things to Taylor. I told her that I had to shout at them so that they would stop.

"I'm sorry the children teased you, Taylor," said Miss King. "It was wrong of them to do that."

Taylor told her that his father lost his job this summer, so they didn't have money to buy any new things for school.

"We can't even pay for our telephone," Taylor added, fighting back his tears.

Miss King gave Taylor a hug. Then she looked at me and told me I was a good friend. She told both of us that things would get better.

Miss King led us into the classroom. As we sat down, she asked everyone in class to please take out their **dictionary.**
She wrote the word "TEASE" in big letters on the board and instructed everyone to look up the meaning of the word.

 I looked through my **dictionary.** I looked as fast as I could. I wanted to be the first to find the word.

I waved my hand wildly in the air to get Miss King's attention, but she didn't call on me. Instead, she asked a girl named Brenda to please read the definition out loud to the class.

"TEASE: To mock someone by playfully saying **unkind** and hurtful things," Brenda read in a loud, clear voice.

Miss King asked the class to think about that. She asked if anyone had ever said **unkind** things to them. Most of the kids put their hands in the air.

Miss King asked them to talk about how it felt to be teased. They all agreed that being teased made them feel awful.

Later that morning, during **recess,** some of the kids who had teased Taylor came to say they were sorry.

After **recess** everyone went back to class. Taylor felt much better now. I felt better, too.

Then Miss King opened a book and began to read us a story.

The story was about an ancient tribe of forest dwellers who called themselves Tree People. She told the class that it was not a true story, but it was based on facts about real tribes.

As she read the story, I **imagined** I was a hunter in the tribe. I **imagined** that at night I slept under the trees.

I **imagined** that I was one of the Tree People.
I liked the story very much. Taylor liked it too.

"The Tree People were very special," Miss King read. "They kept peace in the tribe by coming together every morning at sunrise to sit in a circle under the trees. Each member of the **tribe** would say one good thing about every person sitting there. They called this the **Magic Circle**."

The book came to an end. I wanted to hear more about the **Magic Circle.** I wanted to hear more about the tribe. Then Miss King said that our class was going to become a **tribe** too!

"We're going to be just like the **Tree People,**" she said. "You have one week to find at least one good thing to say about each person in the class. When the week is finished, we will make our own Magic Circle."

It wasn't such a bad first day of school after all. We were going to be **Tree People!**

The next day at school, the class was buzzing with excitement. Miss King gave each of us a small **notebook** with a picture of a tree on the cover.

"It's almost time for recess," she said. "See what good things you can find out about each other and write them down in your notebooks."

   I looked at my **notebook.** I didn't know where
to start. I didn't know what to write.

I was about to give up, when I **noticed** that Brenda had fallen.
She was crying, and holding her ankle. Marcia came to help her,
and David ran as fast as he could to get the nurse.

I wrote it all down in my notebook.

I began to **notice** other things. Some kids were good with animals. Some were good at telling funny jokes.

   For the rest of the week the whole class spent time learning about each other. I discovered that every person was good at something. My notebook was getting very full!

   Miss King reminded us that we would have our first Magic Circle on **Monday** to share all the good things we had learned about each other.

Taylor and I got on the bus to go home. Taylor
sat next to me. He told me he didn't want to go to
school on **Monday.**

 "Why not?" I asked in surprise.

Taylor looked at his toe poking up through the top of his shoe. "What if no one has anything nice to say about me in the Magic Circle? What if they just tease me again?"

I put my arm around my buddy and told him that Tree People were **special.** "They don't tease each other," I said.

Taylor smiled.

Monday morning I jumped out of bed. I was very happy. It was going to be a very **special** day.

Everyone sat in a circle on the ground beneath the shade of the giant oak tree in the courtyard of the school. Each person in the class heard good things about **themselves** and others.

Taylor heard that he was a great soccer player, he was good at math, and he was a great friend. No one teased him.

Everyone really liked hearing good things about **themselves.** And everyone really liked saying good things about others.

"I am very **proud** of all of you," Miss King said. "Now we are all Tree People."

We all sat under the tree for a long time. I sat next to Taylor. I was very **proud** to be a part of his tribe.

If you liked *The New Tribe*, here are some other
We Both Read books you are sure to enjoy!